To Zavier...............................

**with a heart
full of love**
Uncle Jeff, Aunt Jamie,
Becker, Remy & Dustin

Love is all around New York

Published by Sourcebooks Jabberwocky, an imprint of Sourcebooks, Inc.
P.O. Box 4410, Naperville, Illinois 60567-4410
(630) 961-3900
Fax: (630) 961-2168
www.sourcebooks.com

Source of Production: Phoenix Color, Hagerstown, Maryland
Date of Production: August 2015
Run Number: 5004410
Printed and bound in the United States of America.
PHC 10 9 8 7 6 5 4 3 2 1

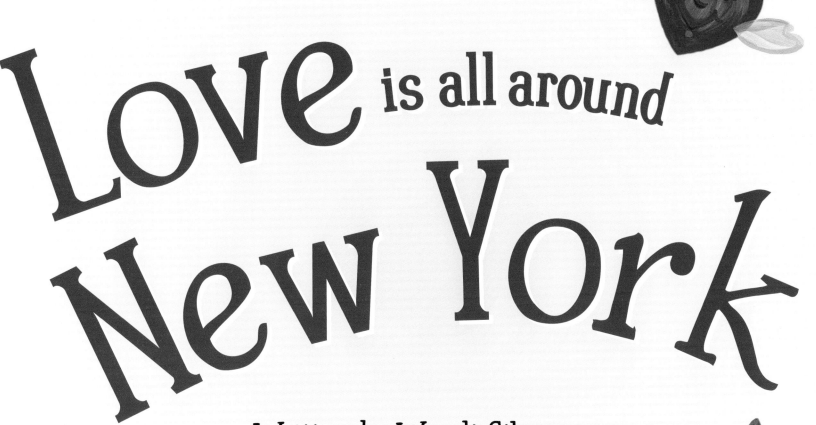

Love is all around New York

Written by Wendi Silvano

Illustrated by Joanna Czernichowska

sourcebooks
jabberwocky

Love is a feeling that comes from **inside.**

Everyone feels it. It can't be denied.

But how do we know that it's there? What's the clue?

How can we **see** it?

Just what can we do?

Love's all around, if you just pay attention,

in people and places too many to mention.

Go look at the **park,**

on the **street,**

at the **mall.**

You'll see love all over. It's **big** and it's small!

All through New York, in cars and on trains,

in taxis and buses, on boats and on planes,

in Albany, Ithaca,

and Syracuse too,

you'll find there is love that will come into view.

Mohawk River

Right there, on the lawn, in grand Central Park

is a mom with her babe,

hearing songs of a lark.

She **swaddles** him, **cuddles** him, **kisses** his ear.

That surely is **love**, it's perfectly clear!

At a store in **Dobbs Ferry**, a girl gets a bear.

She **squeezes** him,

squishes him,

ruffles his hair.

It's clear that she **loves** him. She's **smiling** and bright.
She tucks him in **softly** and **gently** at night.

That same little girl, the very next day,
sees a **friend** at her school who is too **sad** to play.

So she sits down beside him and **listens** and **shares**, making sure that he knows there's someone who **cares**.

Now the boy who was sad feels much better, you see,

so he runs home all happy to play with Magee.

They romp and they frolic.

They fetch and they run.

It's certain he loves him. They're having such fun!

You can see how **love** travels
when **shared** with a friend.
If *everyone* shares love, it never will end.
From one to another, it s p r e a d s and it **grows**.
You can't have *too much*, as everyone knows.

An officer in Yonkers who **helps** change a flat.

A Buffalo fireman who **rescues** a cat.

YANKEE STADIUM

The home team that makes the crowd **cheer** and **clap**.

Each moment has **love** like a **gift** you unwrap.

There's a **father** who sits at the table each night,
helping out with the homework to get it just **right**.
He's tired and busy, but that's **love**, you know…
giving up what you want to **help** someone else **grow**.

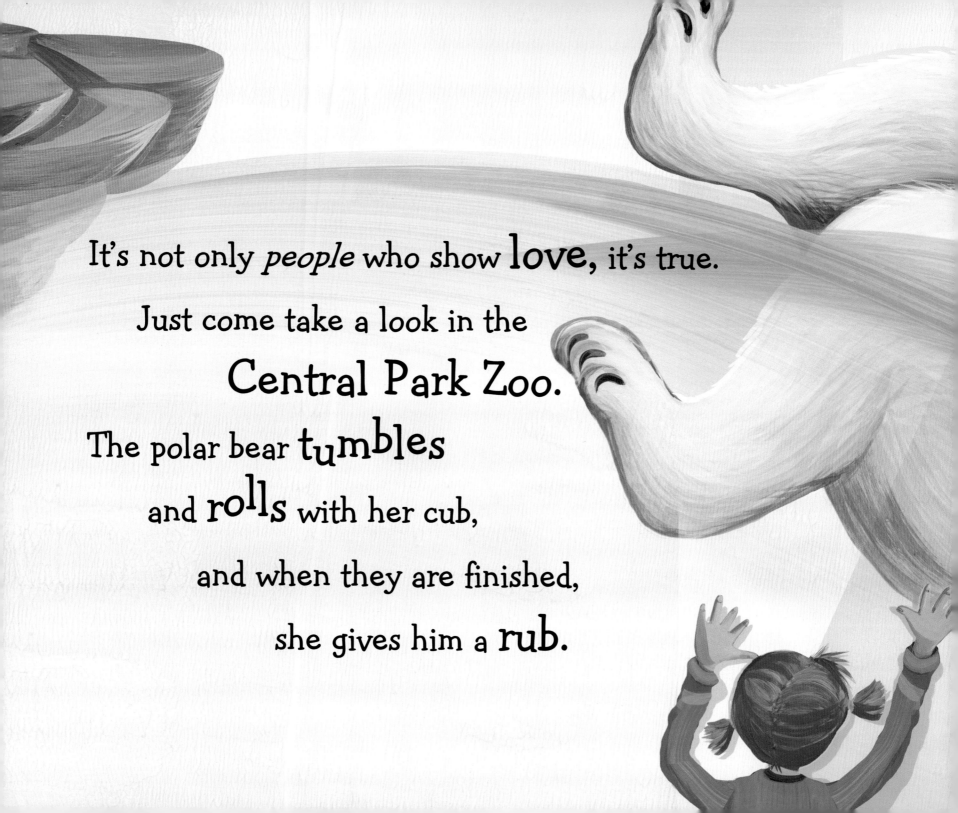

It's not only *people* who show love, it's true.

Just come take a look in the

Central Park Zoo.

The polar bear tumbles

and rolls with her cub,

and when they are finished,

she gives him a rub.

Where else is there **love?** Have we looked all around?

I think we've forgotten—love grows from the ground!

In the **meadows** and **gardens** and parks you will find

that the earth shows us **love** of all shapes and all kinds.

Wherever you look, **love** comes into sight.

It's there in the morning, it's there in the night.

But in all of **New York,**

the best love you'll find

is a **love** that is **gentle,**

and **selfless,** and **kind**...

It's the love found at **home.** It shows up each day
in things people do and in things people say.
There's no greater love, I can tell you, it's true,
than the **love** of your family...

Especially for **YOU!**